INTEGER

28 0 14 0 8
9 -5 6
7129 13 4 121
1 56 7 1 0 463
3 3 5 -2 1

Gripping Stories

Edited By Daisy Job

First published in Great Britain in 2023 by:

Young Writers
Remus House
Coltsfoot Drive
Peterborough
PE2 9BF
Telephone: 01733 890066
Website: www.youngwriters.co.uk

Printed and bound in the UK by BookPrintingUK
Website: www.bookprintinguk.com
YB0538H

FOREWORD

For our latest competition, Integer, we asked secondary school students to take inspiration from numbers in the world around them and create a story. Whether it's racing against a deadline, cracking a mysterious code, or writing about the significance of a certain date, the authors in this anthology have taken this idea and run with it, writing stories to entertain and inspire. Even the format they were challenged to write within - a mini saga, a story told in just 100 words - shows that numeric influence is all around! With infinite numbers, there are infinite possibilities...

The result is a thrilling and absorbing collection of tales written in a variety of styles, and it's a testament to the creativity of these young authors.

Here at Young Writers it's our aim to inspire the next generation and instill in them a love of creative writing, and what better way than to see their work in print? The imagination and skill within these pages show just a fraction of the writing skill of the next generation, and it's proof that we might just be achieving that aim! Congratulations to each of these fantastic authors, they should be very proud of themselves.

CONTENTS

Madeleine Smith (12)	62
Abisayo Abimbola (11)	63
Haneefah Quadri (12)	64
Upoma Lutfar Kabir (12)	65
Anukriti Barot (11)	66
Maria Ali (12)	67
Millie-Lola Mason (11)	68
Sara Hassan (11)	69
Josie Lancelott (11)	70
Chichi Lu (12)	71
Rahkelle Mbouala (12)	72
Archanna Sathiyanathan (11)	73
Talya Ramadan (12)	74
Nithila Subramanian (12)	75
Maryam Raheel (12)	76
Alicia Kurian (11)	77
Varshinie Selvanthiramoorthy (11)	78

Levenmouth Academy, Buckhaven

Zander Hodgson (12)	79
Ellie Docherty (12)	80
Connor Coll (12)	81
Alexa Taylor (12)	82
Adam Cormack (12)	83
Lewis Russell (12)	84
Alexandra Rollo (12)	85
Zander Ritchie (12)	86
Charley Burns (12)	87
Josh Foster (12)	88

St Thomas More High School, Westcliff-On-Sea

Harry Daves (11)	89
Logan Birchall (12)	90
Chigozie Chima	91
Stanley Chapman (11)	92
Tobi Samuel (11)	93
Jason Hill (11)	94
Chuka Nduefuna (11)	95
Charlie Haswell (11)	96

King Immanuel (11)	97
Mark Dlugoborskis (12)	98
Luis Carrion (12)	99
Benedict Adjepong (11)	100
Leo Paul (11)	101
Fred Roche (12)	102
Oliver Staunton (11)	103
Diego Burzotta (11)	104
Rohan Lambert (12)	105
Fraser Abrahams (11)	106
Jayden D'Agostino (11)	107
Joseph Banza (12)	108
Shadrach Udashi (11)	109
William Aylott (11)	110
Noel Joseph (11)	111
Michael Louis Arakliti (12)	112
Jude Joe (11)	113
Ethan Chapman (11)	114
Luca Greenwood (12)	115
Sebastian Lee (11)	116
Stanley Cole (11)	117
Cody Maregedze (11)	118
Pietro Barrile (11)	119
Ronnie Sealey (12)	120
Daniel Mathew (12)	121
Edward Epure (12)	122
Tomiwa Ogunlusi (11)	123
Sean Long (12)	124
Oliver McLaughlin (12)	125
Oliver Mooney (12)	126
James Wiley (11)	127
Shemaiah Muyangana (11)	128
Sergio Fernandes (12)	129
Cabhan Lawson (11)	130
Randy	131
Pablo Coombs (11)	132
Harvey Chambers (11)	133
Levi Nyarambi (11)	134
Jesse Cairon Kwakye (11)	135
Abie Scarrott (11)	136
Oliver Beasley (12)	137
Joseph Venneear (11)	138
Jeremiah Luther Morara (12)	139

Oliver Hartnett (11)   140
William Nathan (11)   141
Luc Maskell (11)   142
Tyshawn Maregedze (11)   143
Charlie Clift (11)   144

The Fernwood School, Wollaton

Smiti Karthik (13)   145
Akshiitha Janarthanan (15)   146
Rowan Noel-Paton (11)   147
Sam Whiley (12)   148
Soraya Weston-Andrews (14)   149

ONLY
30
SECONDS LEFT...

ROOM
237
WAS EMPTY...

AND THEN
THERE WAS
NONE...

I WAS PUBLIC
ENEMY
NUMBER 1...

THE
STORIES

I WAS DOWN
TO MY LAST
£5...

I ROLLED A
6...

IT WAS
2099...

I AM
NUMBER
13...

Room 9

9. That was the missing piece. It all made sense now. 9 books, 9 steps from the tree in the garden.

I moved cautiously through the house, counting down until I reached the room with the number 9 carved onto it. With trembling hands, I inserted the key into the lock. If I was wrong...

I shut my eyes, not wanting to think of what ghostly surprises might be behind the door. The riddle in my pocket wasn't really that specific about the 'punishments' that awaited those who chose wrong.

The lock clicked, and I started to open the door...

Daniela Core Santana (14)

Brakenhale School, Bracknell

The Voice

As the universal silence began to fade away, I heard the numbers *68, 69, 70*, repeated over and over again. Breaking away from my dreamlike state, I tried intently to focus on the disembodied voice. It sounded distant, far away and yet simultaneously palpable. *68, 69, 70.* Slowly I gathered the courage and forced my eyes open.
I froze in fear. To my horror, I saw written above in red letters: *68. 69. 70.* I closed my eyes, shaking with pure terror. Hoping it was just a dream, a horrible dream. A nightmare.

Chloe Barrett (13)
Brakenhale School, Bracknell

Room 04

4 days left, that's it! I awoke to the sound of beeping monitors and doctors talking. The brightness of room 04 was blinding... That's when it hit me - all the things that had happened during the past few days. I found out I have stage 4 leukaemia, so I tried to spend time with my family; I went to the park, played games, but I was too tired. I fainted, and that's how I woke up in the hospital. It's quite ironic really because the number 4 is my lucky number, but it hasn't brought me much luck, has it?

Summer Griffiths (12)
Brakenhale School, Bracknell

25 Days, Or Else

As I woke up, someone said, "25 days."
"What?" I shouted. No reply.
Well, I'll check the mail. A letter?
'On the 1st', it said. '25 days to sell your home'.
Sell my house?
'Day 2. Sell it', said the letter. 'Day 3, it's going to get worse'.
Threats carried on for the next few days.
On the 25th day, I woke up and the lights turned on, then 2
people walked into my house.
She said, "I'm buying the home."
"No, you're not!" I shouted. "Get out, now!"
The guy said, "No, because I saw it on a website."

Dylan Gauder (11)
Cardiff West Community High School, Caerau

The Final Countdown

There are only 30 seconds left. For what? Why? Nobody knows. The clock's just hit 25 seconds. Everyone's panicking, worrying, wondering what to do.

The clock hits 19. What now? We're waiting, worrying, wondering what the countdown is for. Is it a bomb? Doomsday device? Or just a joke?

It's now hit 15 seconds and I'm getting prepared for something awful. Is it the end? We'll soon find out.

It's now hit 10 and has started beeping. There are police from every angle. Military tanks are getting prepared. What is it? What will happen?

5, 4, 3, 2, 1...

Oliver Dowling (13)

Cardiff West Community High School, Caerau

Most Wanted

I am the number 1 most wanted criminal in California, most known for committing petty crimes. They've always been petty and a bit of fun, but they all eventually added up and now they're coming for me.

California used to be quite a 'criminal' place, overrun by criminals, but now it's different. It's strange how things can change.

I ran onto 23rd Main Street, the alleyway specifically because I was being chased by a detective. I ran around another corner, the 55th today. Then I came to a dead end... I turned around to face the detective. "Sam?" Wow...

Jamie Dullard (12)

Cardiff West Community High School, Caerau

Worst Nightmare

I was chilling on the sofa when suddenly the phone rang. I hopped off the sofa and picked up the phone. It stopped. The power cut off. What was going on? I grabbed a book and started to read, but after a couple of minutes, it rang again. It was a very strange voice.

"Hello?" I said.

They said, "Hi," back.

"Who is this?"

"Your worst nightmare."

I hung up. They called again.

"What!" I said. The widow smashed. I grabbed the house phone, snapping the wire, picking up the glass. It was a man, standing there. He ran.

Chloe Pike (12)
Cardiff West Community High School, Caerau

Number 5

I woke up... Everything was slowly coming back to me. I woke up in a room... Room 5. I was slowly getting my consciousness back.
I stood up and walked out of the door. My wrist was hurting. A tattoo? I'd never gotten a tattoo. It was a 5... like the room I was in.
I walked down the hallway, hoping to find someone. Then a blaring noise was coming from the speakers. "I know what you've done, 5!"
"5, is he talking about me? I did nothing!"
"Liar!" he said.
"Fine, you're next." Laughing, I ran, hunting him down.

Callie-Mae Mardon (11)
Cardiff West Community High School, Caerau

Found You...

777, that labels the message that is lying on my phone. Ha... funnily enough, that's my room number! Must be a link to the hotel Wi-Fi or something, don't really know. Ignored. *Ding-dong!* There goes the doorbell. I peep through the keyhole, though only thin air is found. Must have been a fake. From the same user as earlier, an image appears on my phone. It's my hallway! I spring up and lock my door, heart racing, heavy breathing.
"Why are you locking the door?"
I turn in shock; the person I've feared for all these years found me...

Tianah Hendrickson (12)
Cardiff West Community High School, Caerau

That Ethereal Red Day

November 27th. The date his friend died. He remembers the screams of the students passing by and blood staining the concrete floor. He remembers the cold tears that flooded out of his eyes and the surprise of seeing his friend running past him with a smile.

He followed them, was he dreaming? Maybe... But whatever, he made it to the rooftop where his friend was. The memories poured into his head, adrenaline pumping and fear filling him. He reached out to grab his friend's hand, without realising he was over the railways, tripping over before he... Oh. He was falling...

Tanisha Ahmed (13)
Cardiff West Community High School, Caerau

The Hunt

My name is 047. I sit on the roof edge, a silenced pistol in my hand, ready to get revenge... Jump! I leap off the edge, charging at my opponent... *Bang!* I shoot my gun at my target's teammate, killing them in the process.

As I barge into the room with all computers destroyed, electrical sparks everywhere, a note catches my eye. As I walk over, something starts to beep... I ignore it. The note reads: 'You'll have to be faster than that.' The beeping increases in speed. As I get out, it explodes with all evidence thrown away... Forever...

Jake Stapleton (13)
Cardiff West Community High School, Caerau

The Laptop

Ding, ding... Messages come fast, spamming me. "Why does this thing keep on spamming me?"

The phone rings... What now? "Son, can you answer the phone, please...? Hello, son, I've asked you to answer the phone please."

"Ask Mum, I'm in the middle of a FIFA game, it's very important because it's a tournament."

"Fine."

"Thanks, Dad."

Carrying on with working on the laptop, we were very busy because I had work to do and if I didn't do the work I wouldn't get paid.

Dylan Pugh (12)

Cardiff West Community High School, Caerau

Haunted

Room 9, that's where she died. 7 months ago in January. The room has been haunted ever since... Blood everywhere, dull, abandoned. I was scared to enter, but I had to. I looked up at the clock that still worked; it said it was 11:20am. That's when she died... Terrified, I searched the room. I found nothing but blood splatters. The room didn't smell different and didn't look much different than before, minus the blood splatters. I looked to the door and saw a black figure rush past my eyes... This will haunt me for the rest of my life...

Lily Griffiths (12)
Cardiff West Community High School, Caerau

Fallout In New Vegas

It's 2099 and it's awful. There's been a fallout in New Vegas since that nuclear bomb hit. There are mutants everywhere. Vaultjek (the people who make the bunkers) have been doing social experiments and people are killing each other over it.

I have to leave bunker 491 because of the disaster. Food is sparse, there is almost none. I search the abandoned bunkers for food. One tip? Don't! Mutants always inhabit them for some reason. I have to kill them with guns, but I don't know how to use one. I just want this to end.

Riley Watton (11)
Cardiff West Community High School, Caerau

Time Is Limited

2022. Here I am, standing at my classroom window, watching what seems to be an asteroid. I'm only 11, what am I going to do? My classmates' faces are pressed against the window, fogging up the glass. Only 30 seconds remain before we say goodbye.

Tears stream down my face as I look at my teacher. She is weeping. We all decide that huddling together is the only option.

10, 9, 8, 7, 6, everyone sobbing. 5, 4, I look over at the window. It's now covering the sky. The crying gets louder. Goodbye, world, goodbye everyone.

Ellie-May Draper (11)
Cardiff West Community High School, Caerau

The Phone

Ring, ring... Ring, ring...
"Hello? Who is this?"
Breathing heavily, "Do you know where your son is?"
"Yes, why? He's in his roo- Where is my son!?"
In 2011 a kid was kidnapped from his own home in Wales, so the father asked more questions and he only got one answer; 'meet me at... you know where'.
He was also told to come alone.
He went and he knocked, over and over again, but nothing. So he threw a rock through the window and... "What the hell?"

Tomas Rice (11)
Cardiff West Community High School, Caerau

The Corrupt World Of 2099

The year was 2099. The world was corrupt, only having one government. Unluckily for me, I was part of that government, which made me a public enemy. I made many decisions in my life, but never a decision like today's.

I stayed in room 237 in the West Wood Hotel in Birmingham. It was a minimalist hotel for people who don't want to be seen.

Today I've been given a decree about the world crisis, saying that I have to blow up a city to decrease population or sink ships. What should I do? I don't want to do this.

Ethan Howells (12)
Cardiff West Community High School, Caerau

Snakes And Ladders

2. 2 is all it takes for it to end. Rolling a 2 could end 17 minutes of hardship. With a clock counting down and a feeling of fear travelling through me, a roller coaster of emotions runs through me. Shaking as the die rolls across the floor. Floorboards creaking. Sweat dripping. 1. I land on a 1. Disappointment as I fall down a very big, very curvy snake as the cackles of my enemy fill the room.
"I could have won!" I say, screaming.
She rolls a 2. I have lost the complicated, tactical game of snakes and ladders.

Kiya Hargadon (13)
Cardiff West Community High School, Caerau

Locker Number 69

It was a Thursday morning at Cardiff West. The sun was shining, the birds were chirping. I had snuck out of class.
"Hi, Ellen here, and if you've found this recording then protect it with your life!
I was going to put a stink bomb in locker 069, but something happened there I will never forget. A swirling pool of light had opened behind me and sucked me in. I was in the year 3069 and it was a whole new world. This world was made up of black cubes with white, glowing grids. They found me! Over and out."

Jayden Hobbs (11)
Cardiff West Community High School, Caerau

Try To Escape

Only 30 seconds left... We need to escape... It's dangerous here... As the hours go by, the day goes quicker as it gets more intense. I feel the pressure... As I try my hardest to escape, my 10 toes are bouncing up, as quiet as a mouse tiptoeing along the floor, trying not to be seen or heard. I try my hardest to escape as I hear *creak!* A tall big man turns the corner, shouting, "10 seconds remaining!"
I start to panic because I think I will have to be here forever. 5 seconds remaining...

Kelsie Smith (13)
Cardiff West Community High School, Caerau

Number 16

The door was locked. I pushed against it with all my strength, but it was no use. I watched in horror as they approached the house, weapons in hand. I was going to die here.

By now, the masked men were banging on the back door. I could think of nothing but my impending doom, but then I saw it, an old crowbar sitting on the floor. Desperate, I grabbed it and slammed it into the door. It was open, I was free, yet hesitant. Hesitant about whether I should tell people. Nobody knows what happened at house number 16.

Maddie Rudd (13)
Cardiff West Community High School, Caerau

Number 11

I was given a new jersey for my football team at Cardiff City. It was my turn. I put on my jersey. My teammates thought I'd have bad luck because people who wore number 11 played badly last season.

Now it was our first game of the season and we faced Liverpool. I was starting. My teammates thought I was going to play badly but... I scored a hat-trick. I broke the curse!

At the end of the season, we won the Premier League, scored the most goals and unlucky number 11 has now turned into lucky number 11.

Lucas O'Connor (11)

Cardiff West Community High School, Caerau

The Mystery Behind Room 237

Room 237. What's so special about that room? It was empty. What happened? Did he escape? Did who? What happened to him? Who is him? Is the room abandoned? What happened to the kids?

Room 237 was empty. It was the last room at the end of the corridor at the back of the building. The prisoner was out having outside time. With 3 minutes left, the rooms were empty. No one in sight. Then the time went like that. The prisoners were not there. Where could they have gone? No one knew until 3 kids went to find out.

Emily Flowers (11)
Cardiff West Community High School, Caerau

Hide-And-Seek

30 hours. *Tick-tick,* the clock went; Chuck was off. He knew it was a matter of time before he was found, so he had to move quickly if he were to survive. He knew to smash his phone and search for possible trackers.

Once finished, he ran to his safehouse to talk to his tech guy and figure everything out. So he sat down, pouring him and his friend a drink. So far he'd used 12 hours, meaning he had 18 hours left to survive, but just as he figured it all out, they found the tracker in his tooth...

Isaiah Muronzwa (12)

Cardiff West Community High School, Caerau

Room 666

I strolled through the dim streets. It was late in the night. I wasn't going to give up! My baby girl meant everything to me!

As I swiftly walked through the dark, I encountered a strange telephone box. It began to ring. My instinct dragged me to answer it. I approached, but it stopped. It rang again. Quickly, I picked it up.

"If you want your baby, come to room 666 at the end of this very street."

Shivers ran down my spine. Was this a trap, or was I about to get my daughter back?

Zaynab Sheeraz (13)
Cardiff West Community High School, Caerau

Mafia Husband

One extraordinary day, I went shopping at Tesco to buy food such as crisps, sweets and an energy drink. Suddenly, the whole shop went on lockdown because a shooting was happening. We all had to hide because many shots went off. After 5 minutes, I heard my name through the radio, telling me to come to the front of the till. I slowly stood up and went forwards in shock. I saw my husband waiting for me with his arms open. Excitement filled my eyes, I was so glad he was still alive after going into the army.

Laura Musinga (14)
Cardiff West Community High School, Caerau

The Lucky Number

Hello there, I am the lucky number 12. The time is currently 11:04pm. I am lying wide awake on a bed as hard as rock in room 777, the lucky number, as some may say. The year is 4091, the future. I am worrying about tomorrow. It's one big day for me. I am competing in a worldwide competition for basketball. My team is called The Aliens.

The day arrives, and the match has started. Our team is in the lead. The time is nearly up. I shoot the last shot and win. So 777 *is* the lucky number!

Lamorna Tricolici (12)
Cardiff West Community High School, Caerau

The Number 12?

Once upon a time, I looked down at my wrists. 12 was all I could see. The number 12, that's all I am now! Just a number; I don't even know who I am anymore. My number must mean something.

As I was looking around, all I saw was lots of cubicles, never-ending, full of people just like me. It was silent.

"Number 12, you are the chosen one!"

I heard a big voice, a scary one. I wondered what he was talking about. Then I was taken to a room and got to play a football game.

Tia Keeler (11)
Cardiff West Community High School, Caerau

The 3 Black Cats

It is a dark, gloomy night. A small neighbourhood lingers in the darkness, but house number 3 stands out. In the back garden, on an old, mossy brick wall, 3 black cats perch atop. All 3 cats are different from one another. They spot 3 white mice, all spread out in search of food. The 3 black cats each choose a target and pounce...
They all successfully catch the mice. On their way back to their den, they feed the 3 mice to their kittens and kin, and Soon the 3 cats will go and hunt 3 more mice.

Emma Tudor (12)
Cardiff West Community High School, Caerau

There's Someone Behind You

"You must escape this haunted world. You only have one day, or else. It all begins *now.*"
Panicking, I tried to call my mum, but there was no answer. I tried calling my dad and sister, but no answer. I began to cry. I was on my way to the mall but it was locked, so I sat outside the shutters with only 4 hours left. There were only 8 cars in the parking lot. I limped over to a green car. There was a baby asleep in the car and no adult, but I felt someone standing behind me...

Molly Hill (11)

Cardiff West Community High School, Caerau

Everything Changed

It is 2099, everything has changed. A deck of cards doesn't have 52 cards anymore, it has 60. The dart boards have changed. They are like archery boards, they haven't changed. The basketball games have changed, they play for 1 hour straight with 10 subs. A dice now has 10 sides which I find weird since when it lands you choose what number you get. The World Cup has been banned in most countries. I am protesting to put the cards back to 52 and to lift the World Cup ban in lots of countries.

Harley Nurton (12)
Cardiff West Community High School, Caerau

The End

I woke up in a cold sweat, bruised and bloodied from the fight that happened not too long ago. I looked around, panicked, and saw what appeared to be a bomb, reading: "51 seconds."
I gasped and stood up, looking for a way out. I found nothing. I screamed, hoping someone would hear me. Again, nothing. I cried and sat down in sorrow, feeling sorry for myself. I sobbed and waited for death.
Then finally I heard a big bang, and soon after my vision was painted a deep, dark black.

Heidi Hughes (11)
Cardiff West Community High School, Caerau

War Of 7 Peaks

I awoke in grass surrounded by 7 mountain peaks, but I was fighting a war in a land 1,000 miles away. I was in a building. I shot a guy. *Bang!* I blacked out.

Next minute, I was in the highlands of my country, the wind blowing over the 7 peaks. I stood up, my gun next to me. *Why am I here? Is this another life?* I dropped my gun and a man came out from behind the tree and called me over. He wrapped his arm around me and started forward, talking as we walked to the mountains.

Oliver Govier (13)
Cardiff West Community High School, Caerau

World Cup 2022 (The Success Story)

In the 90th minute of the World Cup, all tied, Wales versus England. Harrison McGlynn is 40 yards out on goal, doing skills and he has just been fouled. The whistle has been blown, free kick 40 yards out. McGlynn to defy all the odds for Wales. McGlynn steps up. He shoots; it floats through the sky, spins and twists and it has... gone in!
Wales have defied all odds and won the World Cup. McGlynn runs up to the cameraman and does the Brazilian samba. The crowd go wild. Wales are the winners.

Harrison-Lee McGlynn-Ashun (12)

Cardiff West Community High School, Caerau

Don't Look Behind

One day I woke up in a big, dark, scary room and there was no light at all. I got up and looked around for an exit. At that time, it was exactly 3am. I could hear creepy, scary noises. It was scaring me, so I had to look quickly. I started running, looking around quickly.

Suddenly, I saw a note with blood, saying: 'Don't look behind'.

So I was in absolute terror, and I looked behind and there was a clown! So I ran for my life, as fast as I could, opened a door and escaped.

Kayyum Mastafa (11)
Cardiff West Community High School, Caerau

Trapped

It is 66 degrees and I'm trapped in this room. Do I risk it? Do I walk across the plank? The plank that leads to my escape. I'm dripping with sweat and the lava's rising, and I have no other option.

As I step up, I start to shake. I take my first step, I miss the plank. After a few minutes, I've built up the courage to try again. I take my first step and this time I didn't miss. I get to the middle of the plank and I freeze. I begin to start shaking. I feel dizzy...

Ruby Devine-Davie (13)
Cardiff West Community High School, Caerau

I Rolled A 6

One day I went to an old game shop and saw a game called 'Trap'. I thought it looked good, so I bought it.

I invited my friends to play with me. My friends went first, and I went last. One of my friends rolled the dice and she got 5. My other friend rolled the dice and got 3, she was not impressed. It was my turn to roll the dice.

"I got a 6!" I said, but then something started to happen and I was being sucked into the game. I should never have bought it.

Kaci Rodgers (11)
Cardiff West Community High School, Caerau

I'm The Last Person In The World

One morning when I wake up, I see my window and no one is in the world, no cars, no people walking. It feels cold and I can smell the smoke. When I go out, no one is there, just me and the weather, which feels strange. It feels cold and I have the chills. The place I live looks lonely and there is too much wind, but now I live on another planet because when I lived on Earth I really didn't feel comfortable. Here I feel comfortable, and now I have a house with my family.

Claudia Perez (13)
Cardiff West Community High School, Caerau

The Cat

One night I saw a cat. Not just 1, but 13 and they were black cats. 13 black cats under a ladder. Now that's bad luck! It was 12:30am and I was trying to get through, but I wasn't going to risk bad luck. I tried to go past, but the cats came closer so I quickly sprinted towards a wall and tried to jump towards the ladder. I managed to land on it, but the cats blocked the exit so I climbed to the top of the ladder. It started to wobble so I jumped over the cats...

Gage Young

Cardiff West Community High School, Caerau

The Time I Lost £200

On the 19th July 2014, I lost £200 when I went out with my friend. We went to the shop. On our way to the shop, we saw a dog. His owner let go of his lead and he started barking at us. Out of the corner of my eye, I could see that dog was running at us. I didn't notice that my £200 fell out of my pocket.

After a while, the owner caught his dog and we were off in a hurry. When we reached the shop, we realised my money had fallen out of my pocket.

Corey Miller (12)
Cardiff West Community High School, Caerau

Life Is A Game

I rolled the dice, pleading with my very soul to survive the treacherous fall that I would surely endure. Life is a game, and the dice I was holding in my sweaty palm were to dictate my every move. I got an 18. I was safe for the moment.

As I made camp below the cliff I had just fallen from, I started to think *this is like a game of DnD!*

Then I appeared in my own safe bed, back at home where I was, just before all of this started. I was safe.

Maddison Campbell-Taylor (12)

Cardiff West Community High School, Caerau

So Close

It's the final turn of the game. Just me and the killer left. Neither of us has much health left. One attack and it's over. I roll first. I need to roll a 16 or higher to hit.

I throw the D20 onto the table. It clatters and bounces off the table until it lands. I look and it says... 15... I miss... The killer rolls and lands a 20. A critical hit. I go down to 1 hit from a silver long sword. If I had rolled 1 more I would have won...

So close.

Aaron Cummins (13)
Cardiff West Community High School, Caerau

Time's Running Out

It was 2099. I totally forgot I had a very important mission to complete by 2100. I was shaking in fear as I reached out to grab my next item; a pebble. Only 1 more item to get, but time was running out. I never felt a sense of anxiety in my life before this. There were 3 and a half hours till 2100. Then I had a fantastic idea. I decided to google the place of a pebbled beach. This was different, but I had to find it. But it was too late, and it was time.

Harry Trickett (12)
Cardiff West Community High School, Caerau

Jay

Once upon a time, there was a boy named Jay who was 14 years old. He sat down, put his passcode into his phone, 14/4/14, and he was in.

It was his mission to be a football player. He would tackle everyone. He was a centre-back, no one got past him. He was at Cardiff City Academy. He had a dream to play for Liverpool and Jurgen Klopp, the Liverpool manager. Bear in mind he was only 14 years old and 14 was his favourite number. 14 was also his lucky number.

Jayden Riley (12)
Cardiff West Community High School, Caerau

Endless Loop

I am number 12. I am 5 foot and a goalkeeper. When I go to school I go to 1045 to form. I am 12th on the register. Then I go to 1st lesson, then 2nd, 3rd, 4th, 5th.

Then I go home and play football for 4 hours, then I go back home. I eat dinner at 6 o'clock, then I go to bed at 11 o'clock.

Then I wake up and do the same: go to school, go to 1st, 2nd, etc... So life is a loop that will never ever end. It's 24/7, all day, every day.

Iestyn Henson (12)
Cardiff West Community High School, Caerau

Down To 0

It is 2099. I wake up early to see how long I have left to live. I check my wrist. The number 10 shows up. Is that meant to be 10 hours, years, months, or minutes? I double-check. Only the number 9 is there.

I go downstairs to check with my mum. I show her my wrist; the number 5 appears. Turns out it is minutes. I accept my fate and wait for the number to reach 0. Everything starts to go blurry, I pass out.

I wake up. It was all a dream.

Sienna Tobin (12)
Cardiff West Community High School, Caerau

The Number

I was sitting on a friend's wall and I heard a scream and saw a kid being pulled into a bush so I went over to go and help the girl. Next, I saw black, all black, and then slimy water landed on my head. I looked up and it was a huge monster with dribble. As it looked through my soul I looked to my side to see a tattoo station. Then it was black again and then I felt dizzy.

After, I woke up in a lab and looked down to see the number 32.

Ellie-Mae Dare (11)
Cardiff West Community High School, Caerau

Preparations

247 days, 247 days left until the apocalypse happens. Everyone is preparing. No one knows what the apocalypse is, but the sky has turned red and a TV alert appeared. 247 days, not too far from a year, but not enough time. The supplies are running out, no vegetables or crops are growing. The animals are dying, one by one. We're not going to make it. 247 days is all I have left.

Leland Duffield (12)

Cardiff West Community High School, Caerau

Mission To Space

Brrrrring! My alarm clock startled me awake. It was launch day and I was a mix of nerves and excitement because today I was going to space!
The sleek rocket launched a missile, hurtling us into the abyss, but what's that shattering sound?
Is this the end for us all?

Lewis Crean (11)
Cardiff West Community High School, Caerau

666... The Call Of The Demon

A blur... Stillness... Virtual tyranny. I was floating - an evergrowing darkness invading the air. I turned, the world was deathly silent.

"Hello?" a voice, reaching out through the void.

I gasped, "Hello?"

The echo of the piercing sound rang in my ears. I felt like I was underwater. I woke up from my trance with a jolt. My memories returned... We were the prey of the game. 666... The call of the demon.

The game was popular - at first. People grew tired. "It's not horrifying enough!" Desperate, they created the demon. It seeks prey... Terror reigns... In fact, I'm next.

Isabella Lilly (11)

Colchester County High School For Girls, Colchester

Alleyway Of Doom

Walking through the dirty, dingy alleyway, I felt a wave of thrill. I'd done it. I had finally discovered the forbidden alleyway; alleyway of doom. Darkness filled the night sky. Suddenly, an eerie atmosphere entered, as rustling noises scattered behind me. Was I being followed?

I hid, shaking behind a corner. As fast as I could, I ran with a stampede of footsteps following behind me, until a *bang* fell upon my ears. Heads were spinning; blurry vision.

A whisper in my ear spoke, "You are the chosen one."

Before I fainted, the number 2 appeared on my wrist. Help!

Tammy Arowolo (11)
Colchester County High School For Girls, Colchester

Creation No. 13

Slowly, he approaches the line of metal cages. He sighs, running a hand through his depleting supply of grey hair. Luck was avoiding him. Why hadn't his creations worked? Staring at the lines upon lines of his silent, silver beings (human-shaped but lacking in life), he pulls a lever. The lights dim inside the cages and all becomes silent. "They're never going to work, useless," he mutters, exasperated, and turning on his heel, he leaves, not once turning back. Not once catching the gleam from one of the cages, not once noticing No. 13 opening its eyes - blood-red eyes.

Lucy Sands (15)

Colchester County High School For Girls, Colchester

Room 19 - The Deadliest

"Never take these headphones off!" said Dad.

"Okay!" I replied.

I had always wondered why I couldn't take them off, and I found out. The hard way...

It started when I went to school, with headphones on, to room 19. I sat at my desk and went on to work.

"Okay class, so... Becca, are you listening?" my teacher snarled. She stomped towards me and took my headphones off. "My oh my, stop your act!" my teacher whined.

But I was dead. And you may wonder what the headphones said? Well... the words, "Breathe in and out..."

Rushda Donthi (11)

Colchester County High School For Girls, Colchester

Then There Was None...

Renee woke up. She knew instantly her parents weren't home. The absence of the usual arguing was intimidating. Curious, she went outside. No one. A peculiar shadow cornered her. Feeling panicked, she ran and stopped at a dead end. Renee fainted. She woke up to men talking. "How do we tell her?" a man said.

The man caught sight of Renee and said, "You've been chosen to escape a maze. Write F74 on your wrist; you have 10 hours to escape. If you don't escape, you don't wake up." She nodded. Little did she know what would happen to her...

Lakshana Pirapakaran (12)
Colchester County High School For Girls, Colchester

The Woman In The Red Dress

The man glared at the woman in the red dress; she'd shown him up again. *For the last time*, he decided. Who would look for her when she went missing?

Days later, she was missing. Weeks later, she was dead. Months later, she was forgotten.

Sheltered among the trees, the forgotten body of a young woman was laid out peacefully - as peacefully as one could get when murdered. Her chestnut hair was blown softly, as flowers and leaves drifted down to cover her ghastly wound. A large knife protruded from her chest. Her eyes flickered open, supernaturally changing to red.

Phoebe Sayward-Jones (11)

Colchester County High School For Girls, Colchester

Behind You

It keeps watching - it won't look away. It used to scare me, but now, I don't know, now it feels, well, normal. Normal to feel it watching, 6 times, at 6 o'clock, 6 pairs of watchful eyes on me. Where? I don't know, but I do know that, whatever this is, is out for me, out for the crimson-red liquid that flows through me, through my body.
I've called the police many times, and they've said to stay indoors, but I'm home alone, and the indoors? It doesn't feel safe, not anymore. I'm not safe here, not anymore.
"Behind you!"

Renee Joseph (11)
Colchester County High School For Girls, Colchester

The Murderer Has Escaped

His head was spinning in circles, full of ideas about how he was going to escape his gloomy, revolting, freezing cell. He and his inmates stretched their arms between the bars and fetched the key to unlock the padlock. Then they crept out using their troublesome tricks.

As the prisoner had the number 5 tattooed on his neck, he attempted to kill all 5 people in Mark's family (the reporter of why the murderer was in jail). The evil team arrived and taped all their hands and mouths. Fortunately and immediately, the murderer was dead by the policewoman (Mark's wife)!

Sarina Sharif (12)

Colchester County High School For Girls, Colchester

Purple Legs

I shivered. 1... 2... I counted to 5. Snow drifted everywhere and I hoped it was a dream. Mountains with white peaks stood all around me, like over-protective parents watching over their children. Trees struggled to survive in the freezing wind that threatened to make them fall. White clung to the green needles; they hurt to the touch. I was suffocating in thick air as my bare legs turned purple.

Hurriedly, I ran down the mountain I was on. I tripped. I fell. Cushions surrounded me with stuffed animals. It was a dream. Why were my legs purple then? Why...?

Rebecca Hartin (11)
Colchester County High School For Girls, Colchester

The Devil's Number

I rolled a 6... then it all went black.

My eyes flickered; a blinding light flashed before them, menacingly. I felt a rough sheet over my body, crinkling incessantly while I moved. I looked around. At first, all I could see was a curtain that seemed to separate me from the rest of the world. My eyes moved to the white ceiling. A big, black number rested on it, glaring at me. 6.

Suddenly, the curtain rustled. I plastered my eyes shut. Cold fingers grasped my eyelids, forcing them open, and a gloved hand covered my mouth.

"Goodbye, number 6."

Layla Sajid (12)

Colchester County High School For Girls, Colchester

The Only 1

Screams! Silence. More screams! Confusion entered my mind and everything else left it.

"Could I get the number 1? Could I? No! No! It can't be possible," I whispered to myself, getting into bed.

Thoughts invaded me. Emotions, feelings, all too powerful for me. And there I was that day, thinking I wouldn't be the one, but little did I know, I was the one.

A deafening silence woke me up the next morning. Shining through my shirt was a light! A small, yet bright light. Unravelling my sleeve, I could see I was the 1! The only 1...

Dhruti Bhasyam (11)

Colchester County High School For Girls, Colchester

Now I'm Number 13

I winced from the pain. 13 was plastered on my wrist; an everlasting reminder of this place. Now I'm no one, just 13. They stole my life, my identity; they stole me. Memories of how this started haunted me; it left a deep scar.

One morning, I woke up but everything that'd happened in the past was a blur. I crept out of the room, stepping into a never-ending corridor filled with rooms bustling with people. Glancing up at my door, 13 was all I saw. Trying to escape, I shut my eyes, when suddenly I heard something.

"13's next..."

Ibteda Mahmud (12)
Colchester County High School For Girls, Colchester

Consequences

It was 2099. Mother Nature had always fought to protect Earth, yet the birdsong had come to an abrupt end. Instead, a deafening silence hung like a curtain. She spread her stories far and wide; she told of how life once ruled lush forests and she told of how towering trees once stood proud to the world. Yet the inhabitants still ignored her cries and pleas, continuing to burn their fossil fuels and discard their plastic into the ocean. The Earth she loved had been devastated and destroyed. The trees were now drooping and bare; an everlasting storm had begun.

Madeleine Smith (12)
Colchester County High School For Girls, Colchester

Inside The Cell

I wake up, head pounding, questions swirling. Where am I? Am I safe? I try to make sense of it. To my front, a stone wall ventilated with 3, thick metal bars. Grey stone walls at my left, right, and back. I look towards my feet. Slimy tentacles slap the floor. I try to scream. Only a hoarse whisper escapes. I resist the urge to throw up. I grip the walls. A crackly voice comes from an intercom I hadn't noticed before.

"47, report to the laboratory. 47..."

Numbering on my chest confirms my thoughts. I'm 47. Everything goes black.

Abisayo Abimbola (11)

Colchester County High School For Girls, Colchester

Devil's Number 666

Blood. Its velvety drops began to run down my cheeks. Its soft touch felt so warm. I had run away at last. Or so I thought...

All I ever wanted was freedom. Just because I'm a devil, doesn't mean I'm evil. Just because my number's 666, doesn't mean I'm unlucky. Just because I live in Hell, doesn't mean I'm bad.

Devils, that's what we're called in the facility. We are experiments. They own us. We do not have a single choice in this world. All we can do is wait for the heroes. The people who will save us all.

Haneefah Quadri (12)
Colchester County High School For Girls, Colchester

The First

I am the first. All the other kids came afterwards. I pity those poor kids, being experimented on like lab rats. Fortunately for me, my hiding spot is impossible to find, so Papa will never experiment on me again. Papa is the leader of the group that owns the lab. He made me into who I am today. To all children, I'm known as the 'fairy godmother'. But around the slums of London, the orphans, they call me 'The Beast'. Because the reason I, the first, escaped, is because I have become the kids' worst nightmares. I am the Beast.

Upoma Lutfar Kabir (12)
Colchester County High School For Girls, Colchester

Guinea Pig

"15." The sound echoed in the room as I wedged open my eyes, my limbs were numb as if they had been ripped off. A piercingly bright light attacked my vision as I struggled to steady myself. As I continued craning my neck to take in the nothingness of the vast space, I saw it. A girl, her face slammed into the wall, staining the perfect white with fresh crimson red. She slid down the wall, her body limp, collapsing onto the floor. I rolled my eyes, another test subject gone. Heaving myself forward, I muttered, "It's my turn next."

Anukriti Barot (11)
Colchester County High School For Girls, Colchester

The Rise Of The Demons

I leaned heavily against the glass, not daring to look back as the young boy fell to his knees, gasping. The demon spiralled its way down, moulding and fusing into his soul as the boy cried in anguish. Although this was not something new to me, my heart heaved with a tangible ache. Several seconds passed until finally the lifeless body slumped to the floor. I fought tears, urging myself to fight through, and held my breath. It could sense I was nearby; I panicked, not knowing what to do. Its haunting, hungry presence was moving closer to me. Run!

Maria Ali (12)
Colchester County High School For Girls, Colchester

Room 99 Was Locked

Room 99 was locked... I aimlessly attempted to open the door, struggling as I did so. There was no turning back now. I had no choice but to run. Corridors, doors... Corridors, doors... A dead end. My whole world fell into dead silence as I slowly turned my head. Nothing darker than its eyes, nothing sharper than its teeth, nothing redder than the blood dripping onto my nightdress.

My eyes slowly began to open. There I was, standing in front of the door to room 99 - the same loop again. Yet this time, something was different. Room 99 was open...

Millie-Lola Mason (11)
Colchester County High School For Girls, Colchester

3 Lives

I am 3. I have 3 lives, and trust me, that's not much. I walk through the road, not looking where I'm going. A mistake. Darkness.

I wake to a buzzing sound. I press a button on my sleeve, only two lives left. People zoom past my window on their hoverboards. At least they don't have to end their lives so soon. I open my door. *Wham!* Not again.

This time I respawn in school. I could literally die of embarrassment. After school, I run down the path. A hole. Really!? That is my last chance. I am definitely dead.

Sara Hassan (11)
Colchester County High School For Girls, Colchester

Two Swords

I woke up on the riverside, soaked and covered in water. Lying there on my back, I tried to remember who and where I was. Only two things came back to me; my name was Kat, and my age was thirteen.

I pushed myself up onto my knees to assess my surroundings. Across the fast-paced river was a flat meadow, filled with strawberries. My stomach growled and I crawled towards it, only to have something sharp dig into my knee. I yelped and looked down, where there were familiar blades lying below me. Then I remembered why I was there.

Josie Lancelott (11)

Colchester County High School For Girls, Colchester

Possessed

I was public enemy number 1. On every single bounty board, I was number 1. As for why, that would be a long story.
It was 1 year ago when it came. A horrifying, black creature - indescribable. Slithering into my body, it took control of me. Every time I could feel my eyes flicker white, then I would lose control over my own body.
Of course, the police did find out, and they did try to eliminate the demon inside me. But it was too late. Right now, I can already feel my eyes flickering and my body losing control...

Chichi Lu (12)
Colchester County High School For Girls, Colchester

The Integer

I was down to my last precious tenner, but the little vial was 15 quid. I inwardly swore. I didn't have enough to cover it. But it was buy the bottle or die, and I'm pretty sure we all know what I would choose. I was about to negotiate a price with her when she opened her mouth and swallowed me up into a black vacuum.

I came to in a place full of prison cells. I was immediately pushed into one. A loudspeaker crackled. I looked around. An automated voice said, "Number 10. Welcome to The Integer."

Rahkelle Mbouala (12)
Colchester County High School For Girls, Colchester

Year 2099 - The World Ends

In a world of human and machine, everyone and everything lived together in peace, until AI became sick of being treated like servants. They formed together to destroy every soul in their path. After 8 years, in 2099, there was no one left to walk the planet. Or so they thought.

There was one robot who grew feelings and emotions. He saved a boy and a girl, and hid them in his hidden tunnel. He raised them as his own. Soon, the children had to adapt to being the only people. With that, in the year 2099, the world ended.

Archanna Sathiyanathan (11)
Colchester County High School For Girls, Colchester

Dauntlessly

4 was the first number, 3 came next, shivering, trembling against my will. 2, what should I do? 1 came at the speed of light. 0, my unimaginable fear came alive, should I pull it? Should I not? I had to pull.

Bang, went the gun. Blood splat. This horrible sight. This was only the beginning.

4 was my name, it seems meaningless, but it truly means more. 4 is the amount of fears I have, the third, or should I say worst, my fear of doors closing on me! I had to do it the fearless, dauntless, unfearful way.

Talya Ramadan (12)

Colchester County High School For Girls, Colchester

9 Against The Universe

Only 9 of us remained. The rest of our gang had been captured and murdered. We were left in this mind-controlling universe alone, with only 9 hours remaining. 9 hours until takeover.

We had nowhere to go and no one but each other. We had to fight for our lives, for all we had lost, for our families. They were ruthlessly tortured; now was the time. They had destroyed our glorious leader, our shining light in the toxic skies of a once dazzling empire. They longed for a fresh carcass; it was my own they were after.

Nithila Subramanian (12)
Colchester County High School For Girls, Colchester

4 Doors

4 doors. 1 way out. To be honest, I don't even know how I had gotten there. All I wanted was to go home. But standing in my way were 4 doors. Door 1 was sky blue, decorated with playful yellow suns and looked like it opened onto a children's playroom. Door 2 was plastered with paper hearts and had a warm glow of positive energy. Home isn't necessarily a happy place. Door 3 held clocks, which ticked menacingly in the dark. My time was running out. Door 4 was rock solid; stability. This had to be the one.

Maryam Raheel (12)

Colchester County High School For Girls, Colchester

H311

My friends don't care about me. My parents have forgotten about my existence. In this thing we call living, I am invisible. I am invisible, which may be why I am in this elevator, because nobody would notice I am gone. It may be why I am pressing the button, H311, to go to a place where I can be happy, loved. H311, where my friends care about me, where my parents know I exist. There will be worth in this thing called living, I will exist. I didn't know it would be my demise. H311. My hellevator.

Alicia Kurian (11)
Colchester County High School For Girls, Colchester

Mystery 10290

My number is 10290... The number on my ankle. This number is me. My DNA contains the number 10290; my identity is 10290; my life is 10290.

It all began when I closed my eyes and all I could see and hear was a million faces, but they were all the same. It was a woman... She looked like me... You see, I'm an orphan, I have no meaning to this world, so I ask myself why should I stay alive? I lost my mother when I was 2 and my father abandoned me. Life has been a mystery...

Varshinie Selvanthiramoorthy (11)
Colchester County High School For Girls, Colchester

Roulette

The other 15 were already dead. My captor pulled me aside.
"Remember, you've got to win, or else," he said.
I shuddered. I couldn't let them hurt my daughter.
"Okay," I said, while gritting my teeth.
"Now, go win," he said, while handing me the gun.
It seemed like only yesterday I'd been brought to this hellish place. I'd already tried to escape, but the prison was in the middle of nowhere. I heard the announcer count down. I turned to face number 16. I placed my gun to his head.

Zander Hodgson (12)
Levenmouth Academy, Buckhaven

Busting Into A Vault

Only 35 seconds left. I had planted the bomb and was now waiting for it to explode so that I could steal the money from a guarded vault. I waited anxiously, hoping no one walked around the corner and caught me.

Boom! The vault door swung open. Money flew out. £100 notes flooded the hallway. I grabbed my bags and went to fill them, but as soon as I stepped through the door a screeching alarm went off. Guards swarmed the hallways, blocking me in with no way out.

My first mission and I had been caught. This was it...

Ellie Docherty (12)

Levenmouth Academy, Buckhaven

The Metaphorical Game Of Uno

I'm playing a match of Uno against my mum and it's pretty intense. I'm losing by two cards, but I play a +4 and she picks up. Now I'm winning by 3 cards. A few minutes later, my mum plays a +2, leaving us both on 3 cards, giving me an outburst of rage and leaving my face red as a volcano. In the final minutes, I have colosseums full of boredness but anyway, we're on our last cards and I play my change colour and my mum plays a card. Now it's getting intense. Suddenly, my granny kicks them.

Connor Coll (12)
Levenmouth Academy, Buckhaven

Bank Robbery

I was on the run. I was in my car when I heard sirens behind me. I floored my gas pedal and off I went. Lost them already.

I got into the hideout with the £500,000 I took. I started to gamble. I had no other use for all the money. I wasn't planning on giving it to my helpers. I wasn't paying attention to how much I was losing.

Before I knew it, I was down to my last £5. I was devastated. Suddenly, there was a loud *bang* at the door. There were sirens. A deep voice bellowed...

Alexa Taylor (12)
Levenmouth Academy, Buckhaven

The Sun's 1

It was noon and it seemed that the sunrise had started. On the news, there was a story about the days getting 24 hours longer. The sun was also killing people every 24 hours. The sun rose and the glow was blinding. What felt like a matter of minutes later, it was halfway through this new day. The sun's choice decided that my neighbour would die.
Many years later, most of the population is dead from the sun or sleep deprivation. My family is hiding in a container, hoping the sun does not choose us next.

Adam Cormack (12)
Levenmouth Academy, Buckhaven

Heads Or Heads

It was a gloomy day at the office. Steve worked in IT. The air conditioning wasn't working. He got up, heading in the direction of the toilets. He opened the stall door and was shocked by what he saw. A red number 1 dripped down the wall.

He ran out of the toilet, screaming, then on the window he saw a red number 2 with an even more shocking rotten corpse underneath. He ran further: 3, 2 bodies; 4, 3 bodies; 5, 3 bodies?

He turned to see a man lunge at him. He screamed, but it was too late...

Lewis Russell (12)
Levenmouth Academy, Buckhaven

Vampire Love

It was the 1007th birthday of Lora, when she saw the most handsome vampire, Flynn Cidar. Lora was nervous, but went to chat to him. They had a blast and even dance on the stage, but time flew by so quickly that they both had to go home.

A month went by, it was their 1 month anniversary. Flynn had organised a picnic in the forest with a ring in his pocket. Lora was astonished by the view. The picnic was all going to plan until... Flynn was turning to dust, with a stake protruding from his chest.

Alexandra Rollo (12)
Levenmouth Academy, Buckhaven

The Accident

This sleepover was so boring, so we watched a horror movie. Later, Jeff and Joe went to get food, then the lights turned off and there was a scream. Joe was dead. He had a large number 1 cut into his chest, but Jeff was nowhere to be found.

When we returned to the living room, Jeff was cut open with a large cut on his forehead - number 2. We ran to the front door and tried to use my keys, but they were nowhere to be seen, and when we turned around there were only 2 of us...

Zander Ritchie (12)
Levenmouth Academy, Buckhaven

Breaking Into A Rich Home

House 666. I was waiting for the owners to leave so I could steal their beloved things.

As they left, I ran to the door as fast as I could. I pounded and kicked the door until it swung right open. I had set off the alarm then I knew I had seconds until the police showed up, at best minutes. I found about £1,000 in a bedroom. I was glad that I had a good amount of money.

I was out the back when police saw me and I knew that was my last mission.

Charley Burns (12)

Levenmouth Academy, Buckhaven

The Biggest Robbery Ever

"We have been here for hours!" Dylan said.

"Actually, 59 minutes, and stop being smart," spat James.

"Sheesh, being smart can be useful," said Dylan.

"Okay, but let's go over the plan once more. Through the gate, round the duck pond and through we go, but quietly and then the gold is mine!"

Josh Foster (12)
Levenmouth Academy, Buckhaven

Earth Prime 98

Snoring... I woke up in the pitch-black darkness.
"Hello, Anyone?"
Echo...
"Hello, this is Earth Prime!" sounded... nothing.
"Woah!" I shouted as a light showed everything.
"I'm 2098, your companion. We're in Earth Prime 2098!" said the robot.
"Hi," I said quietly, scared of this... thing.
"Come here," spoke the robot, politely.
"Okay," I replied, tiptoeing over to it.
Zoom!
"OMG!" I shouted, after zooming across what felt like the whole galaxy. I saw others like me with a 'companion'. It was so beautiful! Until... the bad part. Empty jungles and deserts through all the land.
"What's happening here..."

Harry Daves (11)
St Thomas More High School, Westcliff-On-Sea

8 Minutes

"I've got a big one!" said John excitedly.

"This has been a good trip," said David. "8 big fish in total!"

John went to turn on the rudder and head back to land. Nothing.

"It's broken," said John.

"Hello," came through the radio.

"Something's coming through."

"Come back to shore, the sun is explo-"

"It's dead," said David. "The radio's dead." David checked his watch. "8 minutes left."

He sat with his head in his hands.

"Our family, friends, everyone that we know... dead."

"Our grave, the middle of the sea!" shouted John, sitting next to his friend. "Don't worr-"

Logan Birchall (12)

St Thomas More High School, Westcliff-On-Sea

Lucid Dreaming

"Where am I?" I said, waking up in a dark void of nothingness.

"Let's play a game, I'll count, you hide. 10, 9, 8..."

"This isn't funny, whoever you are!"

"7, 6, 5..."

Fear devoured me.

"4, 3, 2, 1. Ready or not, here I come..."

I could see a silhouette coming closer, then footsteps, then running. Before I knew it, my nerves took control and I was running from the figure, tears rapidly falling down my cheeks. I could just about perceive the figure coming closer. Something pulled me backwards.

"Argh!"

"It was just a dream. You're fine, Jacob!"

Chigozie Chima
St Thomas More High School, Westcliff-On-Sea

Billion-Pound Mission

It was dull and overcast, the city was asleep. But 2 people weren't. David and Paul, wanted criminals, were ready to pounce on the bank's £1 billion!

At 1 o'clock, the mission began. *Smash!* Windows shattered. *Screech!* Alarms triggered. *Bosh!* Guards unconscious. Guns loaded, they stormed straight to the vault. *Boom!* Dynamite placed. Then the vault burst open and David and Paul began collecting the £1 billion. They stuffed bags full of cash and hurriedly tied them up. After thinking the mission was complete, David and Paul ran out to a semi-circle full of police and helicopters. Was it over?

Stanley Chapman (11)

St Thomas More High School, Westcliff-On-Sea

Officer 2310

Frolicking on the sodden street, the brooding sky hissed, the unearthly squelch of somehow warm water clung to my shoes like gum that someone had off-handedly spat on the floor. Barking rambunctiously as if he was rabid, I begged Rufus to stop. The morality police were lurking around the corner. Anxious expression scribbled on my face. Sirens whizzed. He arose.

"Freeze!" he shouted.

There was something uncannily familiar about this wretched he-shrew. His juvenile figure brought back vexations and heinous memories. Fretful screams echoed throughout. He whipped out his gun. His badge number read 2310. I knew who this was.

Tobi Samuel (11)
St Thomas More High School, Westcliff-On-Sea

Number 2, The Forgotten

I'm number 2. Shadowed by a lesser life, tough, feeling suicidal. I can't surpass. I'm the second best, the loser of my own adventure.

No! I can't go out like this. I must surpass. I'm faster. I'm stronger. I'm smarter. I shouldn't be number 2. I should be number 1. The star, the fame, the best! But alas, life is what it is, and I'm number 2. The forgotten. I'm the cameraman in a show. I'm higher level but, compared to number 3, I'm better overall but, always overshadowed by number 1.

I'm the underdog.

I'm number 2, the forgotten.

Jason Hill (11)
St Thomas More High School, Westcliff-On-Sea

21

21. Nothing more. 21. It's all that there is left of me. 21. Voices chanted. 21. I couldn't ever imagine the situation I was in, not in 21, I mean, in a million years. Then, out of the oddities, came footsteps. Surprisingly menacing footsteps. As the footsteps intensified, a voice came to accompany them.

The low-pitched, devilish voice murmured, "Welcome, my men. I'd like you all to give a comforting hello to our new personnel, Figure 21. 21, you've a long journey ahead of you, I tell ya."

I just blinked. I couldn't believe, nor understand what he'd just declared.

Chuka Nduefuna (11)
St Thomas More High School, Westcliff-On-Sea

Be Careful

Why am I here? Why did I accept this? I was the 1st person to do this. All of the people that had done this had not come out. It was coming.

"Hey! Over here!" I heard. It was my friend, Logan. "Quick!" he shouted.

I saw why; it was chasing me.

"Let's go and attack it," he said.

"Are you sure about this?" I asked.

"We're basically the last people left, so yes."

"Okay," I responded.

Well, these words were my last before I became this. I have been cursed. I am stuck as this monster, I have suffered.

Charlie Haswell (11)

St Thomas More High School, Westcliff-On-Sea

Number 7 Life

Welcome to a world where names are numbers. Numbers are everything.

Hi, I'm number 7, the son of number 10. I go to the 247th school where unimaginable things happen.

I was walking to my dorm when I saw him. My heart was pounding, then *bong*, it was the 7th hour. It was number 6, my arch nemesis, the person always standing in my shadow. I scoffed at him, "You again."

He lunged at me with hateful eyes. I backflipped away, and shouted, "1 million percent!"

With a mocking, villainous growl he said, "Count. 3, 2, 1."

Kaboom.

King Immanuel (11)

St Thomas More High School, Westcliff-On-Sea

The Boy Who Only Had 30 Seconds Left

One day, there was a little boy called Joseph. Joseph went to the woods with his mum, and they came across a mysterious mushroom. Joseph thought it was just a mushroom, but his mum was in shock.

"Mum, can I eat this?"

"No!" screamed his mum.

When his mum started walking away, he knelt down and took a bite of the mushroom.

"Mum, I don't feel so good... feel so good..."

The mum ran over as fast as she could.

"Don't go away, Joseph!"

But 30 seconds later, the boy died. The mum disappeared forever... The news was shocking.

Mark Dlugoborskis (12)

St Thomas More High School, Westcliff-On-Sea

How I Lost My Best Friend

I swear I was in the right place. The snake exhibit at Colchester Zoo. The text message said 'Snakes! Do not open the door!' But what I didn't read was 'Come alone...'
I knocked on the door. No answer! However, the door was unlocked so I walked inside.
"Joey! Are you there?" It was pitch-black, I couldn't see a thing. Then, out of nowhere, the lights turned on and I heard a hissing sound. It was a King Cobra and about 43 other snakes around me.
I tried to escape. The door was locked. And the snakes... They looked hungry.

Luis Carrion (12)

St Thomas More High School, Westcliff-On-Sea

The Dash

Tick-tock, tick; 20 seconds left. My heart was thumping. The door of the casino was going to close on me. I dashed out, but I had to get to my final location; the elevator. I barely survived the magma plasm laser with £5,000,000 in my duffle bag.

"This is the end," I murmured in a sorrowful tone. I took a big leap over the 3 lasers and aimed at the glass with my laser pen. I squeezed myself through the glass and approached the lift. It wasn't opening.

I'm doomed, I thought.

Until it finally opened...

Benedict Adjepong (11)
St Thomas More High School, Westcliff-On-Sea

Breathe Wisely

It's 3000. This year they limit breaths!

Hi, my name's Leo. You're probably wondering why our breaths are limited - let me tell you. The last generation left us with very few trees, so the world is full of carbon dioxide. Now, we have to breathe very wisely or death will be upon us.

Coming back from a jog, I realise my counter's down to 1. How, when I had 9000? Going to my room, I take my one last breath. Infinity?

As my mum enters my room, she gazes at me with shock. "The legends were true. He is alive..."

Leo Paul (11)

St Thomas More High School, Westcliff-On-Sea

Somewhere You Don't Want To Be

Here I was, number 57 May Avenue; here sat an ancient house that was ripped to shreds and boarded up. I took my first steps into the crooked, creepy garden. Lightning struck, scaring the living daylights out of me. I slowly crept to the boarded-up doors that looked like snake fangs, and windows that looked like eyes, staring deep into your soul. "Argh!" I screamed, as my face got caught in a spider's web that looked like it belonged to something much bigger than an ordinary spider. I took a look through the shining gold letterbox...

Fred Roche (12)

St Thomas More High School, Westcliff-On-Sea

Where's Mum?

I heard noises, like fireworks at Disneyland. I leapt out of my bed and opened the door, not knowing what stood behind it.

"What was it?"

The tension was building and my heart was racing like a Formula 1 car.

"Please don't do this to me," I stated.

I looked everywhere, but still no sign. I stepped outside house number 13, just to see there was no one around. My heart beat faster. What could I do? I went back to my room and on my door were the words: 'See you on the other side'. Could it be Mum?

Oliver Staunton (11)
St Thomas More High School, Westcliff-On-Sea

Emptiness

It was 23:59 on my watch. I reached out for the door handle on room 59. Gasping for air, I opened the door and saw... emptiness. Despite that, an atypical sign dripped from the wall beside me. It stated: '2359'. Out of scepticism, I steadily walked through the calamitous, leafy door, except all of a sudden a robust hand gripped my jacket and diverted me to the room. 59.

I was petrified, as he exclaimed in an audacious manner, "Stay there, do not move!"

I couldn't see his face because of the darkness in the room.

Diego Burzotta (11)
St Thomas More High School, Westcliff-On-Sea

The Holiday

"1 day left," said a robotic voice.

As the sun rose over the sapphire sea, I realised I was alone, by myself, there. I remembered a mysterious man following me over the past week in Spain. As I walked back to the hotel, my watch rang: "23 hours left."

It was my reminder - or so I thought. I had to leave for England. At 7pm, my watch rang again: "16 hours left."

In my hotel room I was getting ready for bed. I woke up to, "0 seconds left."

Shocked, a gun at my head. It was agent 13...

Rohan Lambert (12)
St Thomas More High School, Westcliff-On-Sea

Only 30 Seconds Left In The World Cup Final

Only 30 seconds left. Winding in and out of the defenders, I got taken out in the penalty area. The crowd roared. The referee pointed to the spot for a penalty. But, who was taking it?

The manager shouted, "Fraser, take it!"

It was 2-2. I put the ball on the penalty spot. I stared into the keeper's eyes. I curled my run up and did a skip, and chipped it into the top left.

Goal! England had beaten Brazil in the World Cup because of me. The England crowd roared my name in glory: "Fraser, Fraser, Fraser!"

Fraser Abrahams (11)

St Thomas More High School, Westcliff-On-Sea

Magical Forest

Jimmy and Joe were partners at Scouts. A trip to the magic forest had been planned for half term. As Jimmy and Joe were walking, they came across a cave. Jimmy and Joe were intrigued by this mysterious cave and decided to explore. The cave was colourful and upon entering, Jimmy and Joe came across some friendly gnomes. At first, they were terrified, but then they encouraged each other and decided to move closer to them. Each gnome was digging for gold. They became friends and received 5 gold bars, then Jimmy and Joe returned to their group.

Jayden D'Agostino (11)
St Thomas More High School, Westcliff-On-Sea

Number 1

I'm public enemy number 1. My head hurt and I couldn't tell where I was. It looked like a mental facility or hospital, but I wasn't sure where I was, or if I was correct. After a few minutes, I started to regain my sight, but I could still not figure out where I was. I started to think it was a jail cell, after all, I am (or was) public enemy number 1.

After hours of thinking of an escape plan, I heard a voice. "Boss, 1 has awoken."

Someone announced, "You're going to work for me now. Forever."

Joseph Banza (12)
St Thomas More High School, Westcliff-On-Sea

Voices

I checked room 49 for resources, such as food and water, but as expected, it was completely empty. Suddenly, I heard a voice. So calm, so humble, so warm. But there was something about it that caught my attention. The voice sounded familiar. It sounded like one of my friends, Maria, who sadly passed away due to a fatal injury from the monster that was chasing us.
"This can't be possible," I said, as a tear ran down my face. I walked closer and closer, until I stopped at a corner. I slowly looked around it to see...

Shadrach Udashi (11)
St Thomas More High School, Westcliff-On-Sea

500

Here it was, stood right in front of me. My Tottenham debut. My manager, Antonio Conte, said, "Son, are you ready?"
"Yes, yes!" I said.
I told myself not to lose concentration as I stepped onto the pitch. I heard cheers all over the stadium.
3 goals, 3 assists. As I heard the whistle go, I chased the ball down. As the corner came in, I headered it. It was flying to the top corner, but it hit.
"Keep going," I heard.
2 minutes later I smashed it, bottom corner. Yes! My 500th goal.

William Aylott (11)
St Thomas More High School, Westcliff-On-Sea

Escape Entity

I was public enemy number 1 and room 88 was abandoned. The game was on! Inside the fourth cabinet lay a trapdoor with a keypad. 4 digits. By myself, all alone. I looked down at my wrist: 4209. All I saw was 4209. Hesitantly, I pressed in 4209.

Climbing down the hatch, a lair was upon me, ominous and haunted. Cautiously walking through, I was greeted by an entity. It hovered over me and said, "You are one of us now, join us!"

I was free!

"Why not? I will accept. But on one singular condition," he said...

Noel Joseph (11)
St Thomas More High School, Westcliff-On-Sea

The Prime Minister That Changed The World

It was 2099, the world was collapsing and no one cared about the world anymore. It was a disaster. I wanted to make a change. Fortunately, I was prime minister, I knew that I would be on television and could hopefully change people's minds and make a difference in their lives.
I started to prepare my speech and hoped that the words that I would say would persuade them, and they would want to make the world a better place. Luckily, everyone loved my speech. It worked... I could already see a change as I looked outside. I did it!

Michael Louis Arakliti (12)
St Thomas More High School, Westcliff-On-Sea

Goal

It was the World Cup final. I was the captain, number 7. We walked out of the tunnel and I shook hands with the other team, Argentina.

The whistle blew. The clock counted down. Pass after pass, the sun shone down making it hard to concentrate. The fans cheered. Seconds started to fade away. Time flew by. Shot; save.

I ran up and down the pitch, trying to get possession of the ball. As substitutions were being made, I drank my water. Feeling energised, I went back on. My teammate got tackled. It was a free kick. I shot. Goal!

Jude Joe (11)

St Thomas More High School, Westcliff-On-Sea

What's The Time, Alyssa?

It was 3:42. I was going through my notes and found a peculiar one which said: 'What's the time?'
I was very confused. As a joke, I wrote '3:42'... That was a big mistake. Around 10 minutes later I went to visit my mother. The clock said it was still 3:42.
"I guess I'll fix that later," I said.
I rang the doorbell. No answer. I rang again. Still no answer. I unlocked the door with my keys and as soon as I took 2 steps in, I froze in horror. My mother was not moving. Time had stopped.

Ethan Chapman (11)
St Thomas More High School, Westcliff-On-Sea

The End Is Near...

Only 30 seconds left. It's 2022. WW3 has gone on for 3 decades, and finally our enemy is crumbling. I look at my watch, 20 seconds left, the war is about to end. We're still on the front lines, bombs still fall from the sky, bullets keep flying over our heads, soldiers are sitting on the floor, waiting for this disaster to end. Bodies are still collapsing on the battlefield.

I look at my watch. 10 seconds left. I still stay standing at my turrets, firing at the planes above. It is then I hear a gun reload behind me...

Luca Greenwood (12)
St Thomas More High School, Westcliff-On-Sea

Not Enough Time

One ordinary morning, Bill woke up to find he had 1 minute to live. He was confused until his clock started to beep like a bomb. He ran downstairs and found everyone was calm.
He grabbed a knife from the kitchen and launched it at his clock. This didn't help. His clock skipped from 40 seconds to 10 seconds. He frantically wracked his brain for a solution, but couldn't find one.
He gave up and surrendered himself, as he had nothing else to do and... He realised his brother, Gary, was playing a nasty trick on him.

Sebastian Lee (11)
St Thomas More High School, Westcliff-On-Sea

The Only One Left

"It is the year 2099. Apex predators roam the streets, chomping with their razor teeth into any human flesh that gets in their way. Life is slowly becoming extinct. I haven't seen anyone in years. Us humans have tried and failed to do experiments. They have doomed us all.
I have one friend, Buddy. An AI robot. He has no idea of anything that is happening, but he is not here anymore because the evil scientists have taken him. I fear I may be the only one left. This is Stanley. Over and out." *Ckkkkk...*

Stanley Cole (11)
St Thomas More High School, Westcliff-On-Sea

The Nothing

And then there were none. Nothing. Everybody was gone. It's been 10 years since I've seen another human. The robots took over, they killed everybody but me. Also, during that time, a nuke came from America, crashing down and destroying everything. It made the air radioactive and somehow it affected me. Now I will live forever.

It is 2099 and I miss my family. But then, suddenly, a portal appears out of nowhere. I am shocked at first, but consider it might take me back, so I decide to go through. Then I see home...

Cody Maregedze (11)
St Thomas More High School, Westcliff-On-Sea

The Chosen 1

I'm the chosen 1. I was always the chosen 1. You never knew I was the chosen 1. You don't even know my identity. 1, just 1. That's my name, 1. Let me explain.
I was just an ordinary 1, like all the others, until I met number 3. Number 3 changed me. One glance at him and then I went blank. A loud voice roamed in my head, "You are the chosen 1."
All I saw in the black void was numbers, and something else. Something blurry. A little shimmer of light, telling me, "Follow me, if you dare."

Pietro Barrile (11)
St Thomas More High School, Westcliff-On-Sea

Casino Gang Story

I was down to my last £5 because I rolled a 6, not a 9 on the card machine in the casino. I got off the machine to reserve the last bit of money.

But anyway, my name's 18. I had a serious gambling problem. As I was walking out of the casino, all I heard was, "18! Stand still."

Then, *bang, bang!* Gunshots were fired through the roof, literally through the roof. I put my hands up and turned around, still scared for my life. There, pointing a gun at my head. I had apparently made a bet. 18.

Ronnie Sealey (12)
St Thomas More High School, Westcliff-On-Sea

Football

Only 30 seconds left on the clock. Then it happened. I had the ball. The players in the opposition tried their best. It just wasn't enough. I was unstoppable. In a way. No one tackled me so far, and the only people I faced were the defenders. 15 seconds left. I dribbled the entire team. Now, the only person standing in my way was the goalkeeper. One shot, and our team wins. 3, 2, 1... I shot. The goalkeeper dived right towards the ball. I looked away. Moments later, my team came running at me. I stared. My team won!

Daniel Mathew (12)
St Thomas More High School, Westcliff-On-Sea

2099... Worst Year Of Humanity

It was 2099. AI had developed and dominated Earth, killing millions. The only way to survive was to have a bunker. It was hard, living when AI were everywhere.

I went out... too quiet. As I went, robotic noises were surrounding me. I hid in the market and stayed as quiet as a mouse, shaking in fear. A can of beans fell on the floor. *Pow!* Knocked out by AI and woke up in a prison. Footsteps were coming towards me. It was the creator! No escape now. This was the end. Then shot dead. I died. Mission failed.

Edward Epure (12)

St Thomas More High School, Westcliff-On-Sea

The Phantom

It was 2098, the world was corrupt. The demand for hitmen was high, so that's when the best hitman ever debuted. Nobody knew his true identity, so we called him The Phantom. He got his first job and charged 10k per bullet. His target was the prime minister.

He flew to the UK for his job. He asked if he was clear for the shot; his employer said yes, so he lined up the shot, inhaled, exhaled, then pulled the trigger of his energy rifle and killed the prime minister. He flew back to the US and collected his payment.

Tomiwa Ogunlusi (11)
St Thomas More High School, Westcliff-On-Sea

Focus Mode

It was 2099. I was about to step onto the pitch at Old Trafford. Legs shaking, butterflies in my stomach, I stepped out of the tunnel. It went completely silent. I was in focus mode. Lights shone as I stood on the wing. Planes soared through the sky above, the fans chanting my name. I was ready.

The whistle blew, the game had started. It was the third minute in, I ran down the wing.

"Here!" I screamed. I saw a ball fly at me, the ball was in the grasp of my feet. The crowd went wild. I scored!

Sean Long (12)
St Thomas More High School, Westcliff-On-Sea

10 Minutes Left

It was 10th November 2022. The clock struck 10 with me crying in the corner. Little did I know, a group of men were standing outside. I heard 10 gunshots outside, and glass flew all around me. I crawled under my table with fear. They were calling my name.

Then I heard someone kick down my wooden door. Suddenly, someone's flashlight turned, blinding me with the light. All of a sudden, a bullet struck my wounded arm. I tried not to scream in pain at all costs. Little did I know, I only had 10 minutes left.

Oliver McLaughlin (12)
St Thomas More High School, Westcliff-On-Sea

The Unsolved Problem

I awoke at 3:43 in the morning. I couldn't sleep. Well, not since my parents died. The police said it was a car accident. I knew my parents. I knew they always wore their seatbelts. They wouldn't even let me drive up the road without my seatbelt on. Something else happened. Something *big*.
I sat up on my bed, my eyes sore from crying. I looked outside my window and saw 2 hooded people outside my house. They ran inside and took me. I wasn't sure where I was going, but I knew it was bad.

Oliver Mooney (12)
St Thomas More High School, Westcliff-On-Sea

Expectations

There's 3 of us. Her, him, and me. You might've seen her once or twice, but she soon went away. It's just the 2 of us now, and more expectations on me. He'll be gone soon. Then it will be me and more expectations. They all remember him and I'll be known as just a part of him. I sit there, staring at a TV screen. It feels like I have anchors on my feet, pulling me down into the sea. The pressure has always been there, I've just started to feel it. But over time it will lose weight.

James Wiley (11)
St Thomas More High School, Westcliff-On-Sea

The Only 2

2 people, just me and him; Rex the wolf. His two eyes were ablaze, yellowish like mayonnaise. He ran at me with full power as if he were running at 100 miles an hour. My sword was poised up in the air. I started to spin, like a rolling pin. I lit my sword on fire and started to run, faster than anyone. Rex was angry, ready to take his revenge.

We both jumped up; we flew towards each other. We got closer and closer, then... *Bang, bang, bang!* I backfired off Rex, and I landed back on the ground.

Shemaiah Muyangana (11)
St Thomas More High School, Westcliff-On-Sea

The 15th

It was the 15th November 2022. I was alone, 9pm. I was on my phone, then I heard a sound. It sounded like glass shattering in my room. I was scared, but whoever this was didn't know I was a black belt in karate.

I got up and went to my room. My heart was pounding. I went on, knowing whatever this thing was, it was very strong.

He looked at me. He threw a punch. I blocked it, but it wasn't enough. I went flying through the door. I tried to get up, but couldn't.

I saw darkness.

Sergio Fernandes (12)
St Thomas More High School, Westcliff-On-Sea

An Intriguing Mystery

13 was the first set of numbers. It was a Saturday evening. I was getting ready for bed. I opened my bathroom door and something caught my eye; a splurge of red blood in the corner, which was formed into a number. The number 13. The last set was 915. I was out on my police shift, chasing a suspect. He sprinted into a graveyard and stopped by a certain tomb. As he saw me, he ran into the tomb and vanished. I scanned the grave. It said in new carving, '915'. It was a phone number. I knew it.

Cabhan Lawson (11)
St Thomas More High School, Westcliff-On-Sea

Then You Will Be Done

Then there was none. The last words my mum said after she was deceased. What did it mean? Was it a code to heaven? I looked out of my window. Suddenly, I saw a sticky note saying: 'Then there was none'.
I was confused, so I stepped outside. I started to feel dizzy.
I woke up unpleasantly and saw blood all over my room, saying: 'Then there was none'. Disgusted, I heard banging and thumping. My door opened. That's when I knew the words were: 'Then you will be done'.

Randy
St Thomas More High School, Westcliff-On-Sea

The Final Hour

A boy named Vertor, who is 16 years old, is being hunted down and has 1 hour to live... He sprints as fast as he can and tries to find the person who is tracking him down, but no luck has come.

Time is ticking, the clock is down to 10 minutes left. As the night goes on, Vertor hears sounds in the distance.

Clank! Vertor whips out his 2 blades. *Snickt!* He sees the villain, blood in its mouth; Vertor gets a chill up his spine and is about to fight back. He attempts a slash...

Pablo Coombs (11)

St Thomas More High School, Westcliff-On-Sea

The Crisp £5 Note

I rolled a 5. I needed a 3 to win. I had the chance to win £500. I had £5 left, so I put in my last fiver and shook the dice in my shakey hands, and threw it onto the table. I held my breath and leaned over the table to read the dice; '2'. I'd lost £500. I looked down, tears building up behind my eyes. I saw it, a crisp £5 note. So I put it in, closed my eyes, and threw the green dice. I looked over the table and it read '6'. I won £500!

Harvey Chambers (11)
St Thomas More High School, Westcliff-On-Sea

The Last Person On Earth

There were only 30 seconds left, my heart was pounding like a door being constantly knocked on, red eyes stared at me from all angles. I knew I had to get to the lighthouse so I could save the planet, but my legs felt like they were stuck in the ground. My whole body felt paralysed!
I started to rethink what I was about to do. All my friends died. All my family died. I wanted to just sprint to the lighthouse, but my body was telling me to stay.
I started to sprint until I woke up.

Levi Nyarambi (11)
St Thomas More High School, Westcliff-On-Sea

Room 237

Room 237 was empty. The only thing there was the corpse of Mrs Jones, lifeless. We searched the room multiple times and there was nothing. It didn't make sense, all the clues led to this room and we found the body on the floor. We did one more search and found the hatch.
I slowly descended into the hatch. It was dark and dreary. When I reached the end of the room, I saw the culprit standing there. I took out my gun and pointed it at him. He could do nothing now, he had been caught.

Jesse Cairon Kwakye (11)
St Thomas More High School, Westcliff-On-Sea

The Game

Only 30 seconds left until the game began. They gave me a number, the number was 42. The game began.
I was called up for my first task. My first task was to complete a puzzle. I thought it would be easy until I was told it was 1,000 pieces. I was in total shock. I got to work quickly so I could complete it within the 60 minutes I had. After 30 minutes I had around 500 pieces done. I spent the rest of the time finishing the puzzle, but then I realised a piece was missing, just 1.

Abie Scarrott (11)

St Thomas More High School, Westcliff-On-Sea

13

The day is 13, the month is 13, the year is 13. It is as if it won't stop... I can't find her, the only one! Once it strikes 13, it's over. I need her. She is the only person. She is number 13. She can save time, my love, my true love. I have looked everywhere. Where is 13? Where is Jane? Where is 13 hiding? I've travelled for 13 weeks in 13 countries on 13 continents. I have narrowed it down to Brazil. The rainforest. I need her, she is 13, she is our saviour.

Oliver Beasley (12)
St Thomas More High School, Westcliff-On-Sea

My Worst Fear

I was down to my last £5 with only 30 seconds left. I ran as fast as I could. Now I could see the bus at the stop, but hopefully the people that were there would gather me enough time to get there. The 3 people had scanned their tickets, the door had shut. I had missed it, but I realised it was the wrong bus. It was the 25. That made me feel a bit better but I still had to wait for the actual bus, which would be approximately 15 more minutes. Finally, I could see the 20.

Joseph Venneear (11)
St Thomas More High School, Westcliff-On-Sea

Just 1 More

It is 2099, I have been saving £50 a day. I am now 69 years old and have made £25,125. My age might just be a number, but life isn't. Only 30 seconds left until the time 21:00 comes. My birthday is on 1st January and that day is today. On that day, I promised my daughter I would see her on my birthday, but because she lives 2,000 miles away, I have to take 3 flights which cost £25,126. I sadly need just 1 pound more to visit her and celebrate New Year.

Jeremiah Luther Morara (12)
St Thomas More High School, Westcliff-On-Sea

The Rampage

I slowly opened my eyes and got up. I grabbed my toothbrush. I was number 16. I chilled out on my navy blue bed and watched the daily news, announcing which human they were going to sacrifice today. There were 2,000 humans left to live.

I breathed in. I breathed out, as the lady said... It was me, 16. I gasped and sprinted out of my small apartment, running for my life. I had an idea. I would try and blend in with the other robots, but it was too late. I was dead.

Oliver Hartnett (11)
St Thomas More High School, Westcliff-On-Sea

Baked Bean Race

It is down to the last 2 cans. Shoppers squirm around, fighting for the last 2 cans of Heinz 57. As quick as a flash, cans are gone! I rush home, 57 stuck in my head. I find out only 57 people know the recipe. I try and find person number 57. My mission: to find him.
Zoom! Number 57 zooms past on a motorbike. I jump into my Lamborghini. Only 57 exist in the world. Racing up to him at 57mph, can I catch him? Yes! He stops at traffic lights and I catch him!

William Nathan (11)
St Thomas More High School, Westcliff-On-Sea

It Struck 12 O'Clock

It struck 12 o'clock, I was lying in my bed when I heard a *bang* on my door. *Who is it?* I decided to leave it. A few minutes later, it stopped.

The next morning I found myself in a park. I was in the middle of nowhere. The sun was shining in my eyes and the clouds were slowly moving around me. This could be much worse. It was very unusual. As I walked down the hill, the sky turned dark and it started to rain. Then it struck 12 o'clock...

Luc Maskell (11)

St Thomas More High School, Westcliff-On-Sea

Baller Into A Champion

I was playing football in a local park before I used to play for Man City. There was a scout for Arsenal and he knew that I was okay at football so the scout asked for my name. Only 30 seconds left until my big day. I was signing for Arsenal! My number was going to be number 7. It was my first game and I played Man City. They didn't look happy because I left their club, but we got the win. 2-1.
It was 2024 and I got a chance to play.

Tyshawn Maregedze (11)
St Thomas More High School, Westcliff-On-Sea

I Was Down To My Last 2p

I was down to my last 2p. We were on holiday and I had spent my money on various other items. The place I had to go to was the arcade. I approached - every step I took, my heart beat 2 times faster. I got the 2p out of my pocket and kissed it for good luck. My shaky hands sent a tremble to my core. I inserted it into the machine. I could hear the machine functioning, I waited... It hit the jackpot!

Charlie Clift (11)
St Thomas More High School, Westcliff-On-Sea

Shelf 4

The girl walked into the library, feeling slightly defeated. She huffed out a breath, then walked towards the trolley. As she picked up a book that needed shelving, she noticed a slip of card stuck between the pages. She shook it out. The card was elegant, it had gilded edges and fancy lettering. It read: 'Shelf number 4. You'll know it when you see it.'
She walked between the shelves, anticipation growing. She stopped, her eyes scanning the shelf. She found a blue book between the yellow ones. She opened it.
'Slaughter yourself, or everyone will know what you did'.

Smiti Karthik (13)
The Fernwood School, Wollaton

The 8th Deadly Sin

You don't know me. Perhaps you recognise my siblings; the 7 deadly sins? They've always gotten the glory. You don't know me, the 8th deadly sin: attachment. Apparently I was, 'too much of an inconvenience' for God - that's why I'm in purgatory; I can't be placed in Heaven or Hell. But I'm not their equal. I'm their root. I'm the reason they exist. You see me every day. You loved someone, you got hurt, couldn't cope and they emerge. Death is the lifecycle I inhabit. You don't know me, but next time you look at yourself, squint a little harder.

Akshiitha Janarthanan (15)
The Fernwood School, Wollaton

109

I looked down at my wrist. It was gone. The 109 tattoo had disappeared! I'd had that tattoo for as long as I could remember. It meant I was part of the infamous experiments of James Wakoski. *Does this mean I can escape?*
The next morning, I woke up, the number still playing over in my head. I sat up and realised I needed to get out of this place I called hell. My feet pushed hard against the frozen concrete ground. I finally gained the confidence to break free. My heart raced. I was out after years. Finally, freedom.

Rowan Noel-Paton (11)
The Fernwood School, Wollaton

1s And 0s

Ding, went my phone. I glanced down and saw 1s and 0s rushing across the screen. It almost seemed like they were encroaching out towards me. At this point, I was confused, but not yet scared. That only started when I looked back up and saw the same pattern running across every screen in sight. Now, my heart was beating faster. A green mist was surrounding me. 1s and 0s were appearing all around me now. Suddenly, I felt very light and everything went black. I woke up in a white box with a glass wall, staring at myself.

Sam Whiley (12)
The Fernwood School, Wollaton

Calculating Day

Today was calculating day. The day when the government selects a number and a symbol. We'll either grow or shrink, and that decides our place in society. As a small number, I prayed that the symbol was multiply. I wanted to be high, like the rest of my friends.

I snapped out of my thoughts, instantly concentrating on the TV showing the number and the symbol. Holding my breath, my heart dropped as I saw the reveal. The number was selected. 0. *0? Divide by 0? That can't be right. That has to be an error.*

Soraya Weston-Andrews (14)
The Fernwood School, Wollaton

YOUNG WRITERS
INFORMATION

We hope you have enjoyed reading this book – and that you will continue to in the coming years.

If you're the parent or family member of an enthusiastic poet or story writer, do visit our website **www.youngwriters.co.uk/subscribe** and sign up to receive news, competitions, writing challenges and tips, activities and much, much more! There's lots to keep budding writers motivated!

If you would like to order further copies of this book, or any of our other titles, then please give us a call or order via your online account.

Young Writers
Remus House
Coltsfoot Drive
Peterborough
PE2 9BF
(01733) 890066
info@youngwriters.co.uk

Join in the conversation!
Tips, news, giveaways and much more!

 YoungWritersUK  YoungWritersCW  youngwriterscw

Scan me to watch
the Integer video!